MYTH·MEN™

GUARDIANS OF THE LEGEND

ULYSSES

THE SOLDIER KING

BY LAURA GERINGER

ILLUSTRATED BY PETER BOLLINGER

P9-BZW-243

SCHOLASTIC INC.

NEW YORK TORONTO LONDON AUCKLAND SYDNEY

For Tony, my hero. —L. G.   *For my family.* —P. B.

Text copyright © 1996 by Laura Geringer. • Illustrations copyright © 1996 by Peter Bollinger. MYTH MEN is a trademark of Laura Geringer and Peter Bollinger. • All rights reserved. Published by Scholastic Inc. • Book design by David Saylor.

12 11 10 9 8 7 6 5 4 3 2 1   6 7 8 9/9 0 1/0
Printed in the U.S.A.   08
First Scholastic printing, August 1996

1

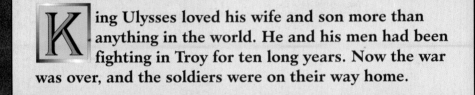

King Ulysses loved his wife and son more than anything in the world. He and his men had been fighting in Troy for ten long years. Now the war was over, and the soldiers were on their way home.

They had sailed through hurricanes. They had escaped from the cave of the Cyclops, a terrible one-eyed giant. And they had run away from the dreamy land of the Lotus-eaters where they had longed to sleep forever.

The soldiers were tired from all their troubles, and hungry — as hungry as hogs. So, looking for a meal and a little rest, they landed in a quiet cove on a small, green island.

Now, on this pretty island
was the palace of a wicked
witch named Circe.

Circe was as beautiful as
she was wicked. Also, she
loved to cook. Blue smoke
rose up from her chimneys,
luring lost sailors to her table.
She welcomed them all — rich
and poor, young and old, big
and small.

In Circe's garden was a magic fountain. Travelers often stopped to stare into its waters. If they stared long enough, faces of wild animals appeared. Fighting men saw fierce lions, tigers, and wolves. Greedy men saw pigs. Clever men saw foxes.

But few were clever enough to know they were seeing their future before them. And fewer still were wise enough to turn back.

Ulysses and his soldiers strode toward the tall white towers of Circe's palace.

Ulysses sensed they were about to face something evil — something with more power to destroy them than all the hurricanes, all the one-eyed giants, and all the Lotus-eaters in the world.

Suddenly, a pack of lions, tigers, and wolves came tearing out of the bushes. The warriors froze in their tracks. Then they turned around and began to run.

All except Ulysses.

The largest lion walked right up to Ulysses and stared fiercely into his eyes. Ulysses stayed perfectly still and stared back. The lion growled. It swished its tail and roared. Ulysses stood his ground.

The lion offered its bushy mane and rubbed against Ulysses, licking his boot. Ulysses patted its head. Then the other beasts gathered around, as friendly as kittens and puppies.

The lion led Ulysses to Circe's fountain. There was the hero's face, reflected in the water.

The moment he saw himself, the water began to churn.

His hair turned red, his eyes turned yellow, his nose turned black and pointy, his mouth turned wide and toothy . . .

. . . lo and behold, he had changed into a fox!

Just at that moment, the sound of a loom from inside the palace filled Ulysses with thoughts of home. He thought he heard his wife, Penelope, singing. As he listened, the fountain stopped churning and the face of the fox faded.

Ulysses looked down at his hands. He touched his eyes, his nose, his mouth. He was still a man. The dreamlike voice hung in the air. It was deep and smooth and it wrapped itself around Ulysses like a heavy mist.

It was Circe's voice.

The witch's song made each man weak with longing. But Ulysses grew stronger as he listened, for his love of his wife and child was so true it gave him strength.

The hero threw open the palace door and led his men into a dimly lit banquet hall. In the far corner, a tall, beautiful woman sat in the shadows, weaving and singing softly. By her side was a long black wand that seemed, in the dim light, to twist and coil like a snake.

While his men rushed to sit around the long banquet table laden with food, Ulysses stepped up behind her and leaned closer to see what she was weaving.

There before him, in a rainbow of threads, were all of his adventures since the Trojan War: Ulysses battling the four winds on the high seas! Ulysses blinding the bloodthirsty Cyclops! Ulysses trapped in the land of the Lotus-eaters!

The longer he stared at the tapestry, the more lifelike the pictures became, until Ulysses thought he would see his future, as well as his past, in the magic cloth. And maybe he would have — but at that moment, Circe turned and their eyes met. She raised her black wand as if to strike him. Instead, she hit the tapestry, and in the spot the wand touched, the cloth wove itself!

4

Circe smiled and led Ulysses to a throne studded with gems. Into a glass reserved for kings, she poured her magic wine.

"Drink!" she commanded.

Ulysses shook his head. In his mind, he clearly saw his wife, Penelope, at the loom and his son playing on the hearth. He wished himself home with all his heart.

Circe waved her wand and three spirits danced forward bearing trays of food, hot from the fire, and more wine. One spirit had sea-green hair. One wore a shroud that looked like the bark of a tree. And the third rained drops of dew from her fingertips. The soldiers grunted with pleasure, taking great big bites of grub and swilling down the wine, but Ulysses refused to eat or drink.

Again Circe waved her wand, and the room was suddenly filled with an awful racket of grunts and groans. "Here are your men, Ulysses!" she said, laughing triumphantly.

Ulysses watched in horror as all his soldiers turned into hogs!

"To the sty, you brutes!" Circe yelled, striking them on their rumps with her wand.

Obediently the hogs stampeded past, their little tails twitching.

Spinning around, Circe struck Ulysses with her wand. "Go join your soldiers in the sty," she hissed. "Or howl with the lions, tigers, and wolves!"

But Ulysses only squared his shoulders and gazed at her steadily, his eyes narrowing. Then he sent his glass crashing to the floor, spilling the enchanted wine.

Again, Circe raised her wand like a whip and hit Ulysses.

NOW LET'S SEE WHAT BRUTE *YOU BECOME!*

For one horrifying moment, Ulysses felt himself changing — into a fox! But the moment passed. The soldier king looked more like a hero than ever. "Wicked witch," he thundered, seizing Circe by the hair and drawing his sword. Ulysses made a move as if to cut off her head in one blow.

Seeing their queen in danger, the spirits fell to their knees, weeping great salty tears.

Amazed that their leader had not changed into a pig, the soldier-pigs squealed shrilly, running around in circles.

And Circe herself let out the longest and most ear-splitting shriek in the history of the world.

When she stopped shrieking, Circe promised to undo her evil spell. Ulysses released her and, dropping her wand, she chanted the magic words.

The pigs rose up on their hind legs. Their snouts grew shorter and shorter. Their hooves turned back into hands. Their mouths grew smaller. Their bristles turned to hair. They began to look like men again.

With a cruel laugh, Circe threw a handful of acorns their way. Before the soldiers could stop themselves, they fell down on all fours and thrust their faces into the floor, rooting for the prize. Then feeling foolish, they scrambled to their feet.

With a trace of a grunt still in their voices, the soldiers thanked Ulysses for saving them. But Ulysses was staring at Circe's wand. It was carved with the heads of animals — the same wild beasts he had met on the lawn outside Circe's palace.

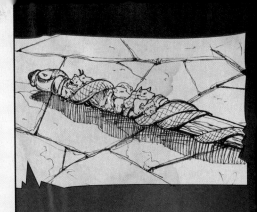

And suddenly Ulysses knew that the lions, tigers, and wolves had all been men once, too.

Ulysses lunged toward Circe's wand. Raising it high, he threw it down as hard as he could, smashing it into a million pieces.

As the bits exploded in all directions, a mob of lions, tigers, wolves, and foxes came crowding through the doors and windows of Circe's palace, changing as they came. By the time they made a circle around Ulysses, each stood on his own two legs. And by the time their cheers ripped through the air, they were men, one and all! They knelt and waved their fists, fiercely hailing Ulysses as their hero.

HAIL ULYSSES!

HURRAY!

But what about Circe?

When her wand broke into a million pieces — the wand that had changed so many men — she herself was transformed. Her arms and legs disappeared, her body grew black scales, and with a horrible serpent's hiss, she slithered out the door, leaving a trail of slime.

Perhaps Circe stayed on her island — a snake for the rest of time. Or maybe she changed again. No one will ever know.

As for her servants: One turned into a tree and took root right there in the hall; one wept until she melted into a sea-green puddle; and the third turned into a cloud that floated out the window and vanished into the air.

And Circe's tapestry? Thread by magic thread, it dissolved into dust. But not before it wove one happy scene — Ulysses coming home at last!

Ulysses hurried back to his ship, hoisted sail, and set off to sea with more men than he had before he landed on Circe's unlucky island.

There would be many more battles to fight, many more dangers to face. But now, more than ever, Ulysses trusted his steady heart to guide him home.

And once he set foot on his native shore, he vowed he would stay there forever — father to his family, king of his domain, and guardian of the legend of the soldier king.